AWAKENING LOVE

CONNOR WHITELEY

No part of this book may be reproduced in any form or by any electronic or mechanical means. Including information storage, and retrieval systems, without written permission from the author except for the use of brief quotations in a book review.

This book is NOT legal, professional, medical, financial or any type of official advice.

Any questions about the book, rights licensing, or to contact the author, please email connorwhiteley@connorwhiteley.net

Copyright © 2024 CONNOR WHITELEY

All rights reserved.

DEDICATION

Thank you to all my readers without you I couldn't do what I love.

CHAPTER 1

"When are you going to get a boyfriend?"

University psychology student Scott Turner sat at a small black wooden table in one of Kent University's many delightful restaurants. He had always loved how many clubs, bars and restaurants the university had catering to all different types of students, there was even a gay club at the uni and whilst he would never ever tell his parents, that was basically the reason why he had chosen to come here.

Thankfully everything else had worked out.

Scott liked this particular Italian restaurant on the campus the best. He enjoyed the creamy white walls that had little pictures of Italy, families and past students celebrating their graduation. He was so looking forward to joining them soon in the summer.

There was soft Italian music playing sweetly in the background that was just loud enough to cut through the chatting, laughing and harsh meetings between the other students in the restaurant, without it being too loud and noticeable.

Scott focused on the two cute men in the circular bar ahead of him. Everyone knew Tom and Bob had been together for years ever since they had first come here five years ago and now they were doing their PhD together. They were so cute together and Scott really wanted that sort of love.

He was determined to find it.

His best friend, Delia, tapped her long red fingernails on the table and Scott smiled at her. She was always more fashionable than him in her long blue jeans, white blouse and expertly done make-up, but he would have been disappointed if her make-up was bad, considering her degree was in special effects.

Scott still enjoyed it whenever she needed him to help her on any coursework. She was stunningly good at what she did.

But he honestly didn't know when he was going to get a boyfriend. He wasn't shy or anything, but besides from the few hook-ups he had in first year, he had been so focused on his degree in his second and final year so far.

It wasn't like there was any shortage of hot men around campus. University seemed to be a breeding ground for hot, fit, young men but Scott just didn't know how to approach them.

He was almost embarrassed by how long it had been since he had asked a guy out, let alone slept with one.

"How about we go down to Brighton or up to

London this weekend?" Delia asked.

Scott smiled but he knew exactly the real reason why she wanted to go. "You just want to avoid your parents coming here,"

"Not true," Delia said, pretending to be offended. "It is just that I don't want to see them this weekend because I want a weekend to myself and they only dropped me back here two weeks ago,"

Scott just smiled and shook his head. He really did love Delia, but he would have loved to see his parents as much as she did. His parents had moved back up North after living down in Kent for all of his life, so they could be closer to his grandparents, but that meant he couldn't see them as much.

He would have loved to see them more.

"How about we make a promise?" Scott asked. "I will do something this weekend towards me finding a boyfriend and you will see your parents. And we can all go out for dinner together,"

Delia frowned. "They do love you. It is a real pain in the ass at times,"

Scott shrugged. "All parents love having a gay son or in your case, adoptive-son,"

Delia laughed. "They bloody would as well. If you wanted them to adopt you they wouldn't even hesitate,"

Scott took a mocking bow. Delia's parents might have been snobbish at times but they were such a laugh, such fun to be around and they were some of the nicest people he had ever met.

But he quickly realised he had not one idea at all what he would do to make good on his promise to Delia.

He had baking society later on so he could talk to Jason, he was hot but had an even hotter boyfriend sadly. And Jason was involved heavily in the LGBT+ society at the university so hopefully they would have something on sooner or later.

Scott really wanted to meet a nice hot guy, not even for sex (but that was always a bonus), but more so he could just be with someone.

Scott couldn't deny that men were precious, beautiful and simply stunning, and he just wanted to be loved and have something more than a mere hook-up. That was probably why he hadn't hooked-up or tried a relationship for two years, because he wanted a real relationship, everyone else just wanted a quick five-minute blast of fun.

And sadly five minutes was all some guys could last. That was always a little sad.

"Anyway, what's this meeting you're having later?" Delia asked. "I have a lecture anyway, we're covering the best way to make fake blood for a budget production,"

"That's a university-level topic?" Scott asked.

"Of course and the main topic takes about ten minutes then we spend the rest of the two hours learning more about the budget film industry. And I need this lecture for my essay," Delia said.

"More power to you," Scott said, he seriously

couldn't imagine anything worst than that lecture. "My meeting's on a two-week research project I'm working on for more research experience. That's when to be a new person joining me too,"

"Man?" Delia said leaning forward and winking.

Scott smiled and shook his head. "Probably nope. The only problem with studying psychology is that it is 90% women and all the men that decide to study it are straight or not my sort of guy,"

Delia shook her head. "You should have done sport science or another sporty degree. It's the opposite,"

Scott bit his lower lip. The sporty guys were hot as hell but most of them were straight, cocky and even if they weren't straight some of them were a little bit too annoying for Scott's liking. But they were probably amazing at sex with their amazing bodies.

"Earth to Scott," Delia said as she stood up.

Scott looked at her and smiled.

"See you later," she said and Scott hugged her tight and as she walked away he honestly had no idea at all how he was going to make good on his promise. He had to get a boyfriend, he just had no idea how to get one.

Not a clue at all.

CHAPTER 2

As much as Joshua Evans loved studying psychology, getting involved in research and helping to advance human understanding when it came to behaviour, he really wasn't sure about his university's bright idea about sending him to Kent University for two weeks to do a research project.

Joshua was normally so calm, confident and collected but as he sat on a warm wooden chair in some PhD student's office with bright white walls, two wooden desks and an entire wall made of bookcases, he was really nervous.

He felt cold sweat drip down his back and his hands were moist. He hadn't been this nervous for years not since his university interview for his course. Granted his own university was only a twenty-minute drive away but Kent University was the best of the best, it was famous for its psychology research and from everything he had seen on campus, the rumours about all the hot women weren't lies.

He was really looking forward to talking and seeing and hopefully flirting with some of the women later on.

The only part of the room that was even remotely remarkable was a strange African bird statue in one corner and Joshua seriously couldn't understand it. He had always liked sculptures and all the girls he had been friends with at secondary school were into art and jewellery and paintings and Joshua had helped them out then, but he just couldn't understand this statue.

It was made from a strange blackwood with little cuts and grooves creating a stunning human-sized bird design. He had no idea why a PhD student would actually want that thing in their office.

It was so ugly but the rest of it was great.

The little hints of tomatoes, pasta and cheese that softly clung to the air made Joshua smile, because if the PhD student he was working with liked pasta as much as he did then he knew they were going to get on great.

He was really looking forward to this opportunity.

Joshua was waiting for Steven Baker to come back from getting the two of them a cup of coffee each. Steven seemed like a good student, a great guy and someone he could easily work with over the next two weeks. But he supposed he was nervous about meeting the other student he was going to be working with.

He had never liked meeting other students because he always felt so inferior to them, his grades were never quite as high as theirs and his parents were never happy unless he got top marks.

But Joshua just wasn't a first-class student and he didn't want to be. He had met first-class students and all they did was spend time in their rooms studying, they lived and breathed their course and Joshua had no problem with that if they wanted to.

It just wasn't him.

He wanted a life, he wanted to meet a cute girl and do amazing things with his life besides from studying. University was about having fun and learning new skills and experiences that you just wouldn't get outside of university.

It was why he had taken his research opportunity after all.

"Here you go,"

The sweet, wonderful aromas of strong but milky coffee filled the air as Steven passed Joshua a large red cup. He liked the warmth that pulsed through him and then he heard other footsteps coming back towards the office.

Steven sat down and Joshua had to admit, even though he was straight as the next man, Steven did look great. He was tall, well-muscular and he probably had a great six-pack under his tight white shirt. The women probably loved him at the university and Joshua supposed a few men might like him too but he had no idea about men liking men.

And Joshua couldn't deny that the small slight beard Steven had really made him even more "attractive" and manly.

Joshua had wondered a few times himself about growing a very minor beard but he just couldn't get over the first few days of not shaving. He knew he was weird but he just felt like he had a fat face if he didn't shave regularly.

His ex-girlfriends had laughed at him, but Joshua knew he was right and had every right to feel how he did.

"We're just waiting for-" Steven said before getting up and going over to them.

"Hello, how are you?" a man asked but Joshua didn't turn around and all his fears, concerns and anxiety flared up as he didn't want the new student to be better than him.

"I'm good thanks mate. You are a lifesaver for doing this for me," Steven said.

Joshua forced himself to turn around and he was shocked. The tall, slim man walking in was "cute", like seriously cute. Joshua had no idea what was happening to him but he could feel his confidence returning, he felt so relaxed and his stomach felt strange.

It couldn't, just couldn't be attraction because Joshua was as straight as both the other men in the office. Yet he couldn't deny that there was something so luring, relaxing and cute about this new man.

It could have been how slim he was without a

gram of fat on his "beautiful" frame, he was a lot taller than Joshua and it showed his long limbs and looked so elegant as the new man walked over and stood next to him.

And the new man's face was very nice too. Joshua liked how smooth it was, there were a few freckles but they only enhanced the natural "beauty" of the man's deep blue sapphire eyes that shone like suns in the dimness of the room. Or maybe the office wasn't dim, the new man was just so bright.

His stomach ached again.

Joshua shook his head because he wasn't attracted to men, he just couldn't be, he loved women and only women. Women were hot, sexy and they were amazing in bed. Men couldn't be any of those things, could they?

"Thank you both for coming," Steven Baker said as he sat down and Joshua realised he wasn't sure if he could survive two weeks with a man that made him feel so many weird and oddly wonderful feelings.

But he had to try.

CHAPTER 3

Scott was so glad that Steven was trusting them to do a quick little bit of research for him to just dot his Is and cross his Ts for his PhD thesis, and he was really looking forward to it. Steven was always a good researcher and he was a great supervisor for Scott's own Final Year Project for his undergraduate degree.

Yet Scott had never known that Steven had amazing tastes in male psychology students. He knew that Steven was sadly straight (and he was seriously annoyed at that because Steven was hot as fuck), but the cute man he was going to be working with for the next two weeks was definitely up there with Steven.

Scott had always enjoyed Steven's office because it was large and tidy and it smelt good, three things that many academics and other university offices seriously lacked. He had been in the offices of other lecturers before and they always smelt so musty, disgusting and not pleasant at all.

It was always so great to get out of them.

Scott didn't want to leave Steven's office, not only because Steven was hot and was a great person, but also because the office was like a little slice of heaven. It was quiet in a university that was crazy, busy and always moving.

And even when he just wanted to find a nice quiet place on campus to talk privately with his friends or academics that he liked on a personal-level, that was always next to impossible.

Steven's office thankfully offered that calmness.

Scott couldn't help himself but smile as he watched beautiful Joshua ask a few questions about the experimental design, variables and how they were recruiting their participants. He definitely wasn't sporty but Scott really couldn't have cared less about that.

Joshua had a great fit body that Scott really wanted to touch, he really wanted to run his fingers over Joshua's soft, smooth, very kissable lips that looked like he would die of pleasure if he kissed. They looked that amazing.

And Joshua looked so wonderful and stunning in his tight black jeans that had allowed Scott to look at his great ass when Joshua went to put something in the bin, and his white t-shirt made him look cute and innocent.

Exactly the type of man that Scott wanted to talk with, get to know and hopefully if Joshua was into men maybe even date.

Scott was impressed that Joshua really knew his

stuff, he knew a lot more than he did off the top of his head and Joshua was asking some great questions. He easily had to be a first-class student or something, so he was stunning, beautiful and intelligent.

Scott really couldn't ask for anything more in a man.

"I'm going to print off the informed consent forms and I'll send them to you now," Steven said, "and then you get just get going on Monday,"

"Thanks," Scott said.

As soon as Steven left the office, Scott felt his face want to break from smiling but he was so glad he was alone with Joshua. He was so cute and hot and he really wanted to get to know him better.

"How are you finding Kent Uni so far?" Scott asked, knowing it was always the safest question to start off with.

Joshua smiled. "It looks massive, and there is so much here. I'm only here for two weeks so I would like to know some tips and things to go to,"

Scott had heard something earlier about Joshua only being here for the research opportunity, something about his university and Kent wanting to become more collaborative. He forced himself not to frown at the idea of not seeing this cutie again after two weeks.

"What sort of things are you into or looking for?" Scott asked.

"I'm into baking but I really want to meet some girls here. Your campus has some great-looking women, don't you think?"

Scott laughed. He wasn't sure why. Maybe it was that his hopes of Joshua ever being into men was now as dead as a doornail or maybe it was because it was cute that Joshua thought he was straight. Scott had always tried to be straight passing because that was the "sort of gay" he wanted to be, but it was always funny when people thought he was straight.

"I don't know sorry," Scott said. "I wouldn't have a clue about how to meet women,"

Scott loved watching it take Joshua's face a few moments to register and then his eyes widened and he started nodding. And then the look of shock and surprise flooded his face.

Scott loved watching straight men find out he was gay because the reaction was always one of two. They were even just shocked and they didn't care he was gay, or they were shocked and they avoided him or made it clear as day as that they were never ever going to be available.

He wasn't sure he understood the second reaction but Scott was gay, he wasn't a slut that wanted to date and do every single man on the planet.

But he wouldn't mind doing Joshua. He was so cute.

"Okay," Joshua said. "Sorry if I looked surprise, it's just I don't meet gay people and I imagined…"

"That we're all feminine and love make-up," Scott said.

"I'm sorry you must think I'm a dick. I'm not

homophobic I promise,"

Scott shrugged. "It's fine honest. We both do psychology we know how powerful stereotypes are,"

Joshua weakly nodded and Scott just wanted to hug him. Joshua looked so cute and vulnerable and guilty but he forced himself not to.

"You said you were into baking?" Scott asked.

Joshua nodded. "Definitely. I love it and don't you find it relaxing?"

"Totally," Scott said and he knew they were going to get on great. "Would you like to come to Baking Society tonight? They would love to have another baker?"

"If you don't mind,"

Scott just nodded. At least he was finally going to be able to spend just a little more time with beautiful Joshua before the weekend ripped them apart.

But even if Joshua wasn't into men, Scott was still really excited for the next two weeks and getting to work with this cutie day in and day out.

CHAPTER 4

Joshua was so amazed after ten minutes of being in the small university kitchen doing baking society with weird bright yellow walls, white kitchen cabinets and a large kitchen island that was meant to look like black marble but it was covered in a cheap cracked layer of plastic.

He was more than impressed that the little university kitchen that was probably meant to be used by eight students working closely together was actually clean enough for baking society. It was definitely part of the learning experience at his university, he had to learn to stomach other people's mess fairly quickly.

He still wouldn't change anything in his life for anyone. The mess and the kitchen and the flatmates during his first year at university was all part of the fun. And he really loved it.

He was standing next to wonderful Scott as he whisked up their bowl of eggs, sugar and flour because they were all making fairy cakes tonight. Then opposite them was a guy called Jason and a woman called Sophia.

Sophia was a great-looking woman with an amazing body, long blond hair and some of the best green eyes he had ever seen. Joshua definitely wouldn't mind talking to her more but she had mentioned her boyfriend a few times, and it was good that she was happy.

But Joshua was surprised that he felt himself recognising that Jason was a great guy too.

Joshua admired Jason's large, broad shoulders and his large biceps showing that he worked out a lot, he was kind, funny and his crewcut really worked.

Joshua was even more confused whenever he saw Jason look at him and smile, his stomach hurt a little and he had to stop looking at Scott to take his mind off it, because Scott's "cuteness" made his stomach really churn.

He had no idea why he was feeling like this, he had never ever looked at men before and he didn't want to start now. But he couldn't deny that Scott made his body react to him.

It was so annoying but Joshua couldn't deny that Scott was a great guy and he was lucky to work with him over the next two weeks.

"All done," Scott said.

Joshua passed him a baking tray lined with pink, blue and purple cupcake liners.

"Thanks," Scott said. "So Jason, I made a

promise to Delia and she wants me to start dating. Help me?"

Jason laughed. "No mate, sorry. All the gays I know are taken, just go to a club or something,"

Joshua gently took the mixing bowl from Scott and he almost gasped when their fingers accidentally touched. He was surprised how warm, soft and perfect Scott's fingers were against his and he started spooning the mixture into the cupcake liners.

He really hoped Scott didn't notice that.

"Can't you come with me? Be my wingman and you might see or make some new friends," Scott asked Jason.

Jason laughed and Joshua liked how they were good friends and he couldn't deny that as much as he didn't want to listen to the conversation because it was useless to him, he was interested to know more about Scott.

"Mate, I have a boyfriend, we don't go clubbing anymore and we're going out for dinner tonight anyway," Jason said.

Scott scooped up a tiny bit of the mixture and threw it at Jason. "You used to be funny before you got a boyfriend,"

Everyone laughed and even Joshua smiled, which surprised him, he never ever imagined he could follow a gay conversation or whatever. And he was surprised how nice it was just being around other men that didn't want to excessively talk about women, sexual conquests or sports.

It was nice just listening and talking about whatever.

"Have you got a girlfriend Josh?" Sophia asked.

"Not yet sadly. Just haven't met anyone special enough, you got any sisters?"

Everyone laughed.

Sophia smiled. "I have but you would have to do a threesome with their wives and husbands,"

Joshua read the room and was glad to see everyone was smiling so he guessed he could make a joke or two despite him just meeting these people fifteen minutes before.

"Happily married?"

Sophia shrugged.

"Good enough for me," Joshua said.

Joshua moved the baking tray over to Scott who was laughing so hard that he fell against Joshua for a moment, and Joshua didn't want to move or anything. He was pleasantly surprised by the warmth of Scott, how good it felt to have his warm breath on his neck and his soft hand touching his arm.

"Oh sorry. Shit forgot who I was with," Scott said.

"I'm fine I promise," Joshua said smiling for a reason he didn't know.

Scott grabbed the baking tray and Sophia took hers and Jason's over to the tray and popped them in.

Joshua looked at Sophia and Scott together, how relaxed they were and that would definitely be the hardest thing about the next two weeks. He wouldn't be at his own uni so he couldn't see his friends like he normally did.

"He's a good guy I promise," Jason said.

Joshua had no idea what he was talking about. "Sorry?"

"I saw how you looked at him just now. Scott is a brilliant guy and he's wonderful-"

Joshua's eyes widened. "No, no, no sorry. You have the wrong idea totally. I'm straight, 100% straight I think I was just surprised he fell on me through laughing so much. I'm not into him at all,"

Jason smiled as Scott and Sophia came over and Joshua couldn't help but think he had just lied but he couldn't be into men. He had loved women for his entire life and it had no sense that he would change his preferences now.

But as the cupcakes cooked in there little purple, red and pink liners, Joshua was looking forward to spending just a little more time with Scott before starting the research project with him on Monday.

It was going to be great fun and Scott was such a great guy. And it wasn't like a straight man couldn't be friends-only with a gay man, right?

AWAKENING LOVE

CHAPTER 5

Scott absolutely loved seeing Delia's mum and dad in a great, huge Mezze restaurant on Canterbury high street. The restaurant was arranged in beautiful rows of long white tables that were large enough to fit a group of people around but not so large that the dinner didn't feel intimate.

Delia's mum was wearing a long middle-eastern inspired dress that might have looked a little weird against her pale white skin but she looked a million dollars. And Delia's dad, well, if he was ten years younger and into men, Scott honestly might have gone for him in his tight black, expensive suit and slight beard. He looked amazing.

Delia scooped up a massive slice of pita bread and rich, creamy hummus and popped it into her mouth. Scott loved mezze food, he loved the rich creaminess of the hummus, the juicy, tenderness of the lamb and the other rich spices that western food all but lacked.

There were people on all the tables and there were a few university students sitting on the table behind Delia. It was clearly two straight couples and Scott had to admit the young man with cute blond hair parted to the right was really hot, but he missed Joshua.

Last night had been so much fun, so much laughter and he had touched Joshua's rough manly hands a few times and he had felt attraction between him. Joshua had walked him back to his university flat and Scott so badly wanted to hug him or kiss him but he knew he couldn't.

He knew that Joshua was certain he was straight but Scott wasn't sure and neither was Jason. Yet he maybe he was just being wishful and hopeful of a future that might not happen.

At least he would have two magical weeks with the wonderful man anyway.

"You still thinking about him?" Delia said passing him a menu.

"I haven't been thinking about him them much," Scott said quickly as her mum and dad debated the wine list.

Delia smiled. "You spoke about him last night when I phoned and I know you better than you know yourself,"

"That isn't hard. Social psychology research says we are terrible at our own self-knowledge," Scott said.

Delia smiled. "You really like you don't him? I haven't seen you hide behind research for years,"

Scott just smiled and finished off his chilli and garlic prawns that he had for his starter, he had to admit the only silly problem with having a best friend you've known from school is that Delia knew him far too well. He loved it most of the time but right now he hated it.

"When are we going to meet your boyfriend?" Delia's mum said.

Scott realised that she must have heard the tail end of that "private" conversation.

"No I don't have one. I just met someone yesterday that I really like, felt attraction between him and he's straight,"

Delia's mum nodded in that wise and regel way that had shocked and scared him when Delia had first introduced him to them (as her boyfriend).

"I have known you a long time little Scott," she said, "and you are rarely wrong about men. Take my husband for instance, you said he was hot one night when you were drunk and you said he was perfectly straight. Believe me, he confirmed it later that night,"

Scott so badly wanted the ground to swallow him up.

"And what about my boyfriend in year 11," Delia said. "You said he was a dick and I climbed up to his bedroom window and found him kissing another girl. You are the perfect sexual detector,"

"Please don't say that again," Scott said smiling.

He knew that everyone at this table loved him but he couldn't be right about this attraction. Joshua was a straight man and he was simply being wishful about what was happening about them.

Scott looked through the menu and was delighted with all the stunning choices for the mains. They normally would have ordered them earlier but Delia wanted to drag out tonight thankfully so she could see her parents for longer.

"What about the pizza?" Scott asked knowing it would annoy Delia's mum.

"Keep saying stupid stuff like that and you'll be paying for all of us,"

Scott stuck his tongue out at her and they all laughed, but as much as he loved tonight and spending time with his de-facto adoptive family, he couldn't help but miss Joshua.

It was stupid because they had only spent a good few hours together yesterday but he was such an amazing guy. He was smart, kind and really hot, and if Scott wanted to love anyone, it would have to be Joshua.

It was just a shame that seemed like a very, very distant reality.

CHAPTER 6

Joshua was so confused as he went into the dull white lab on Monday, 30 minutes before the first participant was meant to show up and found Scott already in there listening to some very good music. This made no sense at all, Joshua was the good student, no student he had ever worked with had turned up before him and it was clear that Scott had been here for a while.

Joshua looked at the "beautiful" man sitting on a blue fabric chair on the other side of the small room and he couldn't believe how much his stomach was filling with butterflies, his throat went dry and his hands turned sweaty.

The small lab room itself was definitely one of the less used ones judging by how new and shiny the two black computer monitors looked on the wooden table to his left, and to his right at the back of the room were all sorts of weird and wonderful neuroimaging pieces of equipment.

Joshua would have loved to explore but he couldn't do that now with Scott being here. What if he didn't know the name or function or something and Scott did, he would look like an idiot.

Scott smiled, turned off his music and pulled out a chair for Joshua.

"Everything's ready," Scott said.

Joshua was shocked. How dare Scott show him up like this and why did his smile have to be so "cute" and why did he have the stupid urge to hug him or something.

Joshua still couldn't believe how he had spent most of the weekend actually missing a man he barely knew. He wanted to call, text or follow Scott on social media just to know more about him.

He was "cute" but definitely not as cute as a woman.

Joshua went over to the chair and smiled at Scott as he checked something on his phone and Joshua checked that everything was right on the computer.

Amazingly enough it was, it was actually more than right, it was perfect. The experiment they were doing involved testing a person in a virtual reality environment and getting them to do a reaction task.

Normally students messed up the software but Scott had done it perfectly, and when he previewed the virtual environment it was so clear, crisp and life-like that Joshua forced his shock not to show.

"What are you surprised about?" Scott asked, and Joshua realised that he said it in such a caring and soft way that he didn't know how to react.

"How did you make it so clear? Is it the software or a setting?"

Scott quickly told him about a special filter you can add if downloaded and install an Add-on and Joshua was amazed. He was going to be popular when he went back to his own university.

"Is there anything else I can do?" Joshua asked, really hoping there was.

"No it's okay. My flatmates were having an argument so I came in early," Scott said.

Joshua felt his breathing quicken at the very idea at Scott thinking he was useless or something and then Scott placed a hand on his.

Joshua wanted so badly to let go, push it away or tell him not to touch him but he liked it. Joshua didn't know why or anything and that was really starting to scare him but he forced himself to smile.

"What's wrong?"

"I'm not useless okay. I am a good student and I came here early today to make sure everything was setup. I am a capable researcher,"

Scott stood up and took his hand away. "I didn't question that at all. I know Steven doesn't choose slackers so I know you're probably the best of the best of the applicants,"

Joshua couldn't believe Scott thought he could only be *probably* the best. Then he took a deep breath of the cold January air and he focused himself to relax.

He knew he never should have quit counselling for his obsession about being the best and how his pushy parents were damaging his relationships.

"No, I'm really sorry. It's just I come from a very pushy family where unless you're a top, top student you're a failure. Believe it or not I am a lot better than I was in secondary school and my early years but I still struggle,"

Scott nodded. "Okay, thanks for feeling like you could tell me that,"

"I could tell you anything,"

Joshua covered his mouth as soon as he said that. He had no idea where it came from, he had no idea why he was so comfortable about Scott.

Scott put up his hands. "Whatever you feel about anything like your pushy parents, you're allowed to feel it. But you don't have to be the best around me, I'm not the best student at all but I like hanging around with you and if it makes you feel better you can set up everything for the next two weeks,"

Joshua was surprised that Scott was being nice to him and it made him respect him even more. Scott really was a great guy.

"What do you say?" Scott asked.

"Yes please. That would be amazing," Joshua said.

"Brilliant. Want to see a cool virtual environment me and a friend made a last summer?"

Joshua loved seeing the excitement on Scott's face so he just nodded and he just knew, truly knew that he was going to enjoy these next two weeks.

It was just a shame that Scott wasn't a woman, because if he was then all of Joshua's dating problems would be well and truly solved.

CHAPTER 7

Scott was absolutely amazed over the next hour at how brilliant Joshua was at everything. He was so welcoming, kind and funny with the participant that they were so relaxed when the headset went on that they didn't even panic like some people did. He had loved creating the life-like virtual environment that sometimes creeped people out because they were so good.

He hadn't done any coding for months and he normally did it with a friend of his that was currently studying in Paris as a part of a Year Aboard programme, but Scott was seriously tempted just to try again anyway.

He leant against the cold white wall of the lab where Joshua led the participant through the experiment, controlling the computer and what the participant saw around themselves.

Scott was impressed that as Joshua's long, sexy fingers artfully danced over the keyboard, he could have sworn that he was falling for Joshua more and more. He was so hot, kind and just an amazing guy.

The first participant they were working on was a short little woman that was so excited about exploring virtual reality that she had almost snatched the headset out of Scott's hand. He loved that there were so many passionate students on his course.

"Thank you for coming. How did you find it?" Joshua asked.

Scott smiled at the participant as she took off the handset and she started telling them how amazing it all was and how she couldn't be happier that she had managed to help us.

He wasn't really sure she needed to be as happy as she was about the virtual reality research, because she was just doing this as part of her course requirements (all psychology students had to in their first and second years), not out of the goodness of her own heart. Yet he still enjoyed seeing how happy she was.

It was that passion she was going to need in the years to come.

"That went brilliantly," Joshua said smiling.

Scott focused on Joshua's stunning smile that lit up the entire lab and he forced himself not to smile himself or go over and hug him. Joshua was just so beautiful and cute and he melted Scott's heart completely.

"Definitely," Scott said. "How do you think her reactions were?"

Joshua laughed, and Scott knew he could never ever get tired of that wonderful musical sound.

He understood why Joshua laughed.

Scott hadn't known before he had checked what environments were loaded into the computer, what they were testing for. Since it was unethical to scare participants for real and it was too uncontrolled to get a real haunted house because there would always be minor, minor differences between the subjects.

Yet if all the scary stimuli were controlled virtually then Scott could easily measure the reaction times, how the eyes tracked the scary objects and things and how the brain reacted to it, because the university was trialling out a new brain imaging VR headset.

He had no idea how it worked but as long as it did the job he didn't care.

Joshua leant against the wall next to him and Scott was really pleased they had ten precious minutes together before the next participant came in. He fully intended to make use of those precious minutes.

"What made you want to do research?" Scott asked.

"I didn't," Joshua said grinning. "I want to get involved in mental processes but I didn't want to be a researcher and I still don't. Next year I'm doing a masters in neuropsychology so studying how the brain impacts behaviour,"

Scott didn't know whether to be offended or not Joshua didn't think he knew what that was. Every psychology student did.

"But my supervisor asked me if I wanted to get some more experience, I said yes and here I am,"

Scott forced himself not to say how happy he was about that, so he just focused on Joshua's soft wonderful eyes that were staring into his.

"I know your uni's twenty minutes away, but do you miss anything? Or what do you want to go back to in two weeks?"

Joshua blinked a few times that surprised Scott.

"I miss some of my friends but I'll see them at the weekend anyway. I don't think I'm missing anything to be honest because I have everything I need right here,"

Scott felt his cheeks flare to live, he felt sweat drip down his back and forehead and he willed his knees not to give out from under him.

"Um," Joshua said, clearly realising what he had just said.

Scott really didn't want to be forceful or something with Joshua, but he really didn't buy that Joshua was perfectly straight or even remotely as straight as he claimed.

As much as Scott prided himself on never pushing or imposing on people, he wanted to say something useful in case Joshua was closeted or questioning or something.

"I'll just say one thing but it's okay to be into men whatever sexuality you want to be. And you can tell me if you're bi or something, I won't be like *go out with me* immediately," Scott said feeling his stomach churn and fill with butterflies.

Joshua slowly shook his head. "I'm not into men,"

Scott wasn't going to protest but even he could tell that Joshua was lying, and that he knew he was probably lying. Scott didn't have a problem with that at all because he knew how hard and difficult figuring out yourself was.

But as there was a large knock on the door and the next participant walked in, Scott couldn't deny that a tiny selfish part of him really wanted Joshua to figure himself out.

Just in case there was a future for both of them. A future he really, really wanted.

CHAPTER 8

Joshua had really enjoyed today and it was only the first day of the research project so he thankfully had another 13 great days working side by side with Scott. He couldn't believe how much fun today had been, talking to participants, helping them through the virtual environment and knowing how much they were enjoying the experiment too.

To Joshua that really was the key to a great experiment, it was all well and good if an experiment created good, high quality data, but if the participants hated it or found it boring then it was always going to fail in the end. Or the data would always be impacted negatively.

Thankfully when it came to virtual reality that wasn't an issue. Especially with "beautiful" and "sexy" Scott by his side and Joshua was really starting to get confused by his "feelings" for Scott.

Joshua leant against the warm kitchen island made from fake black marble in his best friend

Harvey's kitchen. If there was one person he could talk to about his "feelings" about a member of the same sex without it spreading like wildfire it would definitely be Harvey.

Joshua had to admit considering the kitchen belonged to a bunch of university students, it was remarkably clean and rather sterile. The sweet aromas of bleach, orange and cranberry filled the air from someone deciding to clean for a change.

And the brown cabinets sparkled in the bright yellow light from the fake chandelier coming from the ceiling. There weren't many saucepans, plates or much of anything on the black worktops so there had to be an inspection tomorrow.

University students never kept their kitchens this clean.

Harvey normally house shared with ten other people (Joshua was fairly sure that wasn't allowed but it still happened) but they were all at some uni party but Harvey had been great enough to talk to him anyway.

Whilst Harvey finished getting ready upstairs for the party, Joshua couldn't believe he was actually going to have the conversation he had been fearing since Friday.

Joshua didn't have anything against gay or bi people in the slightest, he knew that they were perfectly normal and kind people and the only difference between him and gay people were that he liked women and they liked men. That was it.

But as he knew it was more than that. When he thought about Scott's smooth, slim body against him his wayward parts flared to life, he couldn't stop thinking about Scott and he couldn't deny that he hadn't actually thought about girls too much since he had met Scott.

And he had started noticing how good guys looked too.

It made no sense because Scott was "hot", he was "beautiful" but he was nowhere near what society traditionally thought of as hot. So Joshua had no idea why Scott was having a massive effect on him.

He was perfect though.

"Hi bud," Harvey said.

Joshua laughed as he felt his stomach churn a little, not as strongly as it had for Scott but it still reacted to Harvey.

Harvey stretched a little and Joshua gasped. He could see all the little muscles under Harvey's tight black shirt move, his biceps jerked and his movie star looks were a crime against humanity. He looked great.

Joshua buried his face in his hands. He couldn't bare to look at Harvey as he said what he was feeling.

Harvey came over to him and Joshua rather liked Harvey's strong manly earthy aftershave. It smelt nice, attractive.

"What's wrong bud?"

"I... how do you feel about men liking men *and* women?" Joshua asked still not daring to look at his best friend.

"Oh," Harvey said.

Joshua's heart beated faster and he was so glad he wasn't looking at Harvey anymore.

"How did you know?" Harvey asked.

"I might have met someone," Joshua said relieved how nicely and naturally the words rolled off his tongue.

Harvey laughed. "Bud I think we're talking about different things,"

Joshua stood up perfectly straight and smiled at his best friend. "Sorry you first,"

Harvey shook his head. "I'm bisexual and I told a bunch of our uni friends today so I didn't know if they told you,"

Joshua grinned. "No of course not but that's great. Good for you,"

Joshua hugged Harvey and he had to admit that hugging a man was something he never ever would have done before. He never would have wanted to do something like this because it wasn't a "manly" thing to do, but right now just hugging Harvey (non-sexually) felt okay.

Nothing bad was going to happen to him and this felt right.

Harvey broke the hug. "Thanks Bud and I'm still with Jasmine and she is great, supportive and she's even given me permission to physically try out my *new* sexuality, but I won't do that. Men are hot but I love Jasmine for now,"

Joshua could only nod. That was basically what

he felt, he still loved women and he still wanted to enjoy them but he just couldn't get his head around the idea of liking men.

This was the first time it had ever happened in his life.

"How did you figure it out?" Joshua asked.

"It takes time," Harvey said. "I watched a lot of YouTube videos about bisexuality, I couldn't talk to anyone about it because I don't know any bi people but you have me now,"

Joshua was really glad about that and he was sure he was going to make good on the offer.

"But honestly, it takes time and you cannot rush these things. You need to figure out what you like and what you don't like,"

Joshua nodded. "When did you become so wise?"

Both of them laughed and Joshua knew he wasn't going to figure this out for a while because he had 13 days including a weekend to enjoy "beautiful" Scott's company.

He fully intended to make good use of that time and he really hoped that by the time the experiment was done, he would have figured himself out.

And hopefully "sexy" Scott would be there when he did.

CHAPTER 9

Scott was so pleased with how the experiment was going after three full days and as he started the experiment with the last participant he was so excited for the end of the day, especially because he really wanted to ask out Joshua to a restaurant or something. Delia had been dying to meet him after all.

Sexy Joshua was leaning against the bright white walls of the lab and he looked stunning in his tight blue jeans, crisp white shirt that Scott so badly wanted to run his hands down and his sapphire eyes were simply amazing.

Scott went over to the computer and started the programme. He had already given the instructions to the participant, a tall thin woman with long brown hair, about how she would find herself in a forest that was gradually getting darker and darker as the sun was setting.

It was probably one of his favourite virtual

environments because Scott flat out wasn't a horror fan but he did love virtual worlds.

On the computer monitor he could see what the participant was seeing and in a few moments a massive Bigfoot would jump out at them.

So far every single participant except one had screamed so loud that Scott had laughed so much no sound came out.

He loved being a researcher.

Joshua came over to him and Scott didn't know what had happened Monday night but it was good seeing him so happy, cheerful and relaxed.

"Do you think she's a screamer or not?" Joshua asked.

"I think so,"

Scott looked at the monitor for the exact moment. The massive Bigfoot jumped out and the woman waved.

"Well that wasn't what we wanted," Joshua said so quietly Scott strained to hear him.

Scott only nodded. It was true but that was why he liked researching, he never knew what he was going to find.

"You're really good to work with," Joshua said.

Scott had no idea where that came from. "Thanks so are you,"

Joshua looked like he was weighing up telling him something, and Scott didn't know where to press or not.

The computer monitor clicked a few times to let

him know that the virtual environment was about to run out so he queued up the next environment.

The woman screamed.

Scott hadn't had a participant scream at a pile of dolls in the middle of the forest yet.

"Relax you are perfectly safe. I'm here and remember you can come out and end the experiment at any time," Scott said calmly and without any judgement in his voice.

"Na it's okay. I can continue," the participant said.

Scott loved hearing that.

Then the forest environment changed to an abandoned factory. All of the environments looked exactly like the real things at the moment but it was the final one of a normal house that they were interested in because the aim of the study was to find out about fear in everyday places.

Like the home.

Scott went back over to the computer monitor and looked at beautiful Joshua as he smiled like he was now ready to tell Scott what was going on.

"I think I might be bi," Joshua said.

Scott's heart leapt up to his throat. His stomach filled with butterflies. His wayward parts flared to life.

There was actually a chance he could be with sexy Joshua.

But he needed to play it cool.

"Okay. Thanks for telling me, I know, I really know it's a big step and as I said before I'm going to give you your space but if you need any help about figuring out your sexuality I'm here for you,"

"Thank you," Joshua said, "and that's why I'm telling you. Can we, I don't mean this as a date at all, go out for dinner or something so we can talk,"

Scott really loved it when things came together because he could finally kill a few birds with a single stone. He had been wanting to meet up with Delia for dinner anyway, she had been wanting to meet Joshua for ages and Joshua wanted to talk to him.

And chances are he would be more comfortable if a straight woman was there anyway.

"Do you like Italian food?" Scott asked.

Joshua bit his lower lip. "Pasta, tomato sauce and real Italian flavours?"

"Of course,"

"Definitely," Joshua said.

Scott could have sworn he heard the participant smile slightly as she went onto the last environment and whilst her being slightly distracted might have impacted their data slightly, Scott was seriously looking forward to getting a much more precious type of data.

Data on how Joshua felt about men and hopefully if there could ever be a chance that the two of them could be together. Something Scott wanted more and more with each passing day.

CHAPTER 10

Joshua was so glad he had agreed to go to dinner with "beautiful" Scott at the Italian restaurant on campus. It was a lot nicer than anything at his own university with its bright walls, very cute female waitresses walking around in their tight black uniforms and rows upon rows of tiny black tables.

Everything at his university was so large and long that these little tables just seemed alien. Joshua really liked that, it was different, refreshing and it was why Kent University was apparently the best one.

The entire place smelt great with velvety hints of tomato, bacon and cheese that smelt just like the summer he had spent in Rome. The entire restaurant was so perfect that Joshua knew that he was going to love the next two weeks and he was certainly going to have to visit Kent University afterwards, even if it was just for the food.

There were tons of students of all different ages, heights and degrees of fashion that varied as much as the course everyone was doing. They were all chatting, walking about and some silly people were knocking off mugs unfortunately. They were clearly the early drunks.

Joshua didn't care about them.

"This is the famous Joshua," a woman said as she sat down next to Joshua.

He just looked at Scott and presumed this was Delia, Scott's best friend that he had mentioned was joining them. And he was never going to mention it but he really wanted to have a woman with them.

He didn't want people to think that him and Scott were on a date or anything. He wanted anyone who looked at them to think he was as straight as an arrow, and he had jokingly heard before that being bi was the worst sexuality of them all because no one believed them. If you were with a guy everyone thought you were gay, if you were with a woman you were only straight.

Joshua preferred people to think he was the latter for sure.

"I see why Scott's excited about you,"

Scott coughed and Joshua smiled. It was "cute" seeing him embarrassed and Scott was a great guy and really, really kind for agreeing to have this conversation with Joshua.

Joshua just hoped he wasn't going to regret it.

After a quick round of introductions, Delia waved over a waitress friend of hers and they all ordered. Joshua was flat out looking forward to his vegan pizza with extra cheese, one of his favourite dishes in the entire world. He was really glad that Scott was having the same.

"So you think you might be bi?" Delia asked.

Joshua wanted to nod but he felt himself shake nervously and he started tapping his foot on the ground. He subtly looked around to see if anyone had heard, he didn't know why he was checking but he just did.

"It's okay," Scott said quickly.

Delia nodded. "Sorry I was being forward. Is there anything you want to talk about?"

Joshua couldn't believe that these two people were being so nice to him and he was so lucky that a guy like Scott wanted to spend dinner with him. Scott really was a prince amongst men.

"Yeah," Joshua said forcing out the words. "How, how did you, you know, know you liked other people that might not have been women?"

Delia looked at Scott. "I'm straight so you're up,"

Scott smiled. "I don't know really. I know it's a process but I realised when I started noticing everything my friends said about girls, I found with boys. Like she's beautiful, she's fit, she's got a great ass. I was always thinking he's beautiful, he's fit and he's got a great ass,"

Joshua looked down at the table. That all made sense and he had always been able to appreciate a good-looking guy because there were some men that did look really, really good. He had never thought of that as a sign of him liking men.

"Can I ask why do you think you're bi?" Scott asked.

Joshua smiled at the hot waitress as she gave them their drinks of diet cokes without ice. He wrapped his hands around the perfectly cool glass.

He didn't want to tell Scott he thought he was bi because he thought Scott was hot, sexy and damn well beautiful. And that even realising he meant every single word of it was scary as hell.

Why couldn't he just be straight?

Joshua hated how the idea of being anything other than straight was scary as hell. What would his friends think? What about his parents? What about all the comments he might face in the future?

No it was all too much.

Scott reached across the table and loosely gripped his hand. "Is everything alright?"

Joshua nodded and he really enjoyed the warmth and softness of Scott's hand in his. It felt so natural, so calm and so right that he really didn't want this moment to end.

"Here's your pizza," a waitress said.

Joshua jerked back and he felt his cheeks burn hot. He really hoped the waitress didn't get the wrong idea, as much as he might like the idea of being with Scott he didn't want people to think that, for now at least.

As the waitress placed their pizzas in front of the three of them, Joshua looked at how elegantly, cute and perfect Scott looked as he sliced up his pizza like an expert.

If he was bi then Joshua knew Scott would be the perfect guy to be with but he was scared. He knew that, he hated he was scared and he doubted that Scott would ever want a guy like him.

Scott was perfect, beautiful and he must have had tons of experiences with guys before, so Joshua had no idea at all what he could offer Scott that past men couldn't.

And that thought killed him inside.

CHAPTER 11

Scott couldn't believe how amazing the pizza was, he had always liked vegan food because it always tasted the same as "normal" food. The cheese was so creamy and clean-tasting, the fake ham was juicy and crisp and the crust was so soft that it was so much nicer than biting into the teeth-breaking hard crusts that so many other pizzas seemed to love.

And the entire night was perfect so far. Scott really enjoyed spending time with Delia after she had isolated herself for the past three days working on her Final Year Project. She was working on creating an ambitious design portfolio thing for a fantasy film set using all of her make-up and special effect knowledge.

Scott had no idea what it was actually about but that was how he thought of it.

Joshua had been really chatty. Scott always liked hearing him laugh, seeing him smile and just spending time with him was so relaxing. Scott hadn't felt this great in months and it was all because of Joshua's positivity.

"And that's how I first picked up a girl," Joshua said as him and Delia laughed so hard they were crying.

Scott hadn't followed the conversation too well but he didn't care. He was spending time with the man he really, really liked and it was good news that Joshua and Delia got on so well. Scott was more than glad the past wasn't going to repeat itself when he got with a guy and him and Delia hated each other.

That was just a nightmare and ultimately why the relationship failed. But Scott so missed the sex.

"How's the coursework coming?" Scott asked. "You need my help again?"

Scott noticed how Joshua sat up perfectly straight. He knew that Joshua suffered from bad anxiety about university life and he was obsessed with being the best but he shouldn't feel the pressure with Delia, surely?

She was on a different course for starters.

Joshua's phone started ringing. "Sorry I have to take this?"

"Sure," Scott said. "I'll miss you until then,"

Scott wanted to die of embarrassment as soon as he said it but Joshua gave him a beautiful smile and Scott just watched him walk away. He was so cute.

"He's amazing. Please get with him, love him and marry him," Delia said.

Scott smiled. "Calm down. I made you a promise to get a boyfriend and that's what I might be doing. I don't know but I really like him,"

Delia took a massive sip from her diet coke. "He is brilliant but why did he get so shifty when you mentioned coursework?"

Scott didn't like it when Delia was so observant. He had no idea how the women missed the Shard (the UK's tallest building) when they went to London but she could notice something as small as that. Women were mysteries he was just glad he didn't have to discover.

"From what I gather he comes from a very demanding family where unless you're achieving top marks, you're a failure. And I think that scares him," Scott said really feeling for Joshua.

"That sucks," Delia said. "He must know he's brilliant,"

Scott nodded but he wasn't so sure about that. He knew from his mental health classes that there was a massive difference between acknowledging when someone told you you were great and actually believing it deep down.

Scott doubted Joshua believed how great he was. He was going to tell him that as soon as he got back.

"And can my friends borrow you again please at the weekend?" Delia asked fake smiling. "They need some subjects to dress up as knights and they want to paint blood and everything,"

Scott mockingly rolled his eyes. "I thought I was done with fake blood after first year. Why can't your friends paint my arm and make it look like a branch or something?"

Delia laughed. "Because I'll do that for you later if you want and then I'll make photos for my website,"

"Thank you," Scott said poking his tongue out at her.

Scott smiled even more when Joshua came back, sat down and weakly smiled at him. Scott really enjoyed looking into Joshua's stunning eyes but he was surprised by the sadness in them.

"Who was that?" Scott asked.

Joshua's face was stone. "My parents said they're going up North for three weeks on Monday because my brother won a major award at his university for developing some new cancer treatment,"

"That's great," Delia said.

Joshua shook his head. "They want to see me first and catch up before they go,"

"That's not great?" Delia asked.

Scott didn't know what to say. This had to be Joshua's worst ever nightmare seeing his parents before they go up for a massive award ceremony or whatever they were doing, all whilst Joshua was doing someone else's research.

"I'll come with you," Scott said not having a clue what he was signing up for.

"Me too," Delia said.

Scott had no idea why Delia had said that but he loved her anyway.

Joshua looked unsure but Scott mockingly

fluttered his eyelids a few times and Joshua smiled. He was so cute.

"Fine, thanks both. I'll send you the details,"

"More important question," Delia said. "What should we have for dessert?"

Scott laughed because that was a very serious question. What could three very hungry university students devour after a great meal?

AWAKENING LOVE

CHAPTER 12

It turned out the answer was tiramisu, one of Joshua's favourite desserts, and two nights later Joshua was even more amazed that Baking Society was making the English version, they were making trifle from a pack. Nothing could be easier than placing the lady fingers in a bowl, soaking them in some liquid and setting some jelly on top all before Joshua's favourite part that involved a lot of cream.

He was sort of waiting for the gay creaming comments between Jason and Scott, but oddly enough he was really looking forward to them. He supposed he just wanted some gay banter.

The kitchen they were in had to be Joshua's personal favourite out of the two he had seen so far. It was a massive kitchen that could easily fit ten or fifteen people in with black cabinets, a dull grey floor and an entire wall was made up of nothing but floor-to-ceiling windows.

The windows gave Joshua a great view of the rest

of the campus that had so many buildings over such a large distance that the edges of the buildings looked like a mini city in the darkness.

It looked great and homey and Joshua loved being here.

It was even more homey with all the other students around the large black table talking and doing the "cooking" together (making a trifle was more assembly job than cooking) and Joshua didn't understand why some students were wearing a pink pin but they looked good.

"How's the experiment going?" Jason asked wearing some jeans, black shoes and a black t-shirt.

Joshua had to admit it was a shame that Sophia wasn't there this week but she had some deadlines to finish up.

"Great thanks," Joshua said. "It's a lot of fun, Scott's wonderful to work with and life is great,"

Scott elbowed him and Joshua didn't regret what he said at all. The first full week of them working together had been wonderful and with the heating being broken yesterday, Scott had jokingly come into the lab wearing shorts so Joshua got the pleasure of seeing Scott's long sexy legs all day.

And that memory had lasted long into the night.

"Definitely," Scott said. "We're getting some great data and I'm looking forward to next week,"

Joshua nodded. He felt the exact same way and Joshua liked everything about this week. He really liked baking society, he seriously liked Scott and he had to admit he was the happiest he had been for years. He felt like his true self.

He knew that was a silly way to put it but he couldn't deny how much his stomach churned and filled with butterflies when Scott bend over to look at the computer monitor or whenever he laughed or whenever he did anything.

"How's going the hunt for a boyfriend?" Jason asked Scott.

Scott laughed. "It's going very well, well maybe,"

Joshua so badly wanted to say something but Scott was perfect and he fully intended to ask him out next Friday. At least if Scott rejected him then they didn't have to see each other again.

But Joshua really wanted to explore his bisexuality and there wasn't anyone better than Scott.

"I heard you're roped into helping Delia and her friends out," Jason said. "I'm jealous,"

"Same," another student said. "That make-up peeps always have the fun projects,"

Joshua couldn't agree more and if him and Scott did end up going out together he was looking forward to seeing Delia more and learning from her.

"Then we're seeing my parents," Joshua said.

"Meeting the parents already," Jason said grinning. "That's a big step don't you want to wait a few more weeks first?"

Joshua frowned as he realised that Jason thought him and Scott were dating. He might have wanted that but he didn't, he couldn't have other people thinking that.

He didn't know why but his heart pounded in his chest. Sweat poured down his forehead. He just couldn't have people thinking that.

Joshua reached for a lady finger but he accidentally crushed it in his hands.

"You okay?" Scott asked.

Joshua shook his head. "I am, it's just I don't like the idea of people just assuming we might be together,"

He felt so guilty as Scott took a few steps back.

"Wouldn't you want to be with me?" Scott asked.

Joshua wanted to shout out yes, hug him and maybe if he had enough courage think about kissing him, but something stopped him. He didn't know what but he couldn't say the words.

Scott folded his arms. "Can I talk with you in private?"

Joshua slowly nodded really hoping he hadn't undone all the good work he had done the past week. He liked Scott way too much to spoil it all now because of his own stupid fears.

Scott went out of the kitchen and Joshua followed him out into the long dark blue corridor outside.

Scott leant against the wall. "Let's get something straight right now, because every time I think we're getting close or you're accepting yourself you seem to react,"

Joshua nodded. He had no idea what to say.

"Are you scared about being bi? I understand this is a learning curve but, you know Jason was just joking right?"

Joshua took a long deep breath and he looked at the ground. He couldn't bear the thought of seeing Scott's disappointment.

"I am scared and I don't know why. I've never met another gay or non-straight person before you and everyone's new. I don't know how my friends would react, how my parents would react but yes… I, I might like you,"

Scott placed a soft wonderful finger under Joshua's chin and lifted it up gently.

"That's okay," Scott said. "I know what it means to be scared but you are brilliant, amazing and whatever you need to tell yourself so you're okay you can do it. But know I like you, a lot,"

Joshua smiled as soon as he heard that. It was amazing to know that Scott liked him and he was patient and he was the most wonderful man Joshua had ever met.

"I like you too but, can we not do anything on these feelings until after the research please?" Joshua asked. "I promise we can ask each other out next Friday just not before,"

Scott nodded. "Sure, and I guess that gives you more time to figure yourself out,"

Joshua hadn't thought about it like that but he had been meaning to do some research on being bi from other bi people over the weekend, so Scott was right, as always.

And as Scott led them both back into the kitchen, Joshua was so excited about next Friday because it was going to be amazing. He was going to have a boyfriend and that excited him a lot more than he ever wanted to admit.

CHAPTER 13

Scott was so relieved that the wonderful, beautiful and sexy man he was seriously starting to fall for was into him too. That was the best news he ever could have hoped for and now he was looking forward to 6 days' time even more.

Scott had to admit that Joshua's parents had great taste in restaurants as him, sexy Joshua, his two parents and Joshua's best friend Harvey sat around a large round table with a white silk tablecloth, a few elegant tealights in the middle and the sweet aroma of mint filling the air.

Joshua's parents were almost as stunning as their son. Scott was impressed with his mum's long sweeping black dress that looked like it should be in a Hollywood production instead of being in Canterbury and Joshua's father looked like the CEO of a massive international banking firm worth billions of pounds.

And then there was Joshua in just a crisp white shirt, black trousers and he had his arms looking like trees.

Both of them did.

Scott had always loved how brilliantly Delia managed to do make-up, special effects and she always said she could transform anyone into anything. And she was always right but given how the make-up and other substances used were water and sweat resistant so they wouldn't run off or lose their effect halfway through a production, they were stuck with them for the next six hours.

A little fact that had never remotely bothered Scott until now, and judging how Joshua's parents were hardly speaking as they studied their menus like exam papers, he supposed it bothered them a little.

"You must be proud of Joshua," Scott said. "He's one of the best students I've met, he's a hard worker and my supervisor wouldn't just pick anyone for his position,"

"Hm," Joshua's mother said without batting an eyelid.

Scott looked over at Harvey, who was cute as hell and openly bi, and he just shook his head. Scott knew Harvey didn't want to continue the line but he was sort of committed now.

"What's your proudest achievement?" Scott asked Joshua.

Harvey shook his head and Scott instantly knew this was going to end very badly but he was committed now.

"Probably my essay last month on Psychosis. I

out an 88 out of 100,"

"Your brother would have gotten 98," Joshua's mother said. "Maybe if you spend less time doing make-up you would be a better student,"

Scott gasped. "I'm sorry but an 88 is amazing I wish I could have those sort of grades but a 72 is all I can manage,"

And Scott really didn't care about that, 72 was an amazing grade that he got occasionally but Joshua's parents didn't need to know that.

Joshua's father put down the menu and frowned at his son. "What score did you get for that poster presentation you needed to do? It was nice seeing how excited you were over Christmas,"

Joshua frowned. "68,"

Scott was so jealous, poster presentations were the worst assignments ever, he hated them with a passion.

His mother shook her head. "Your brother would have done better,"

Scott just glared at her. "I'm sorry, but this is not your other son. Joshua is an amazing student, an amazing person and, who cares if he doesn't get the best of the best grades? He is still going to live an amazing life,"

Joshua's mother glared at Scott and Scott didn't back down for a second. Everyone else at the table picked up their glasses of wine or coke and took small sips.

"We are the Evans Family and we only get the

best," his mother said.

"And maybe you are the one who is a failure of a mother for pressuring their child too much. Joshua loves you, he gets anxiety attacks at the idea of failing you. You are ruining his life,"

Joshua gasped.

"Maybe he should get anxiety attacks for failing us. He is automatically a failure by failing to get into Oxford,"

Scott shook his head. "There is more to life than reading papers and being a student. And anyway, who the hell are *you* to judge academic success?"

Joshua's father looked furious. "We are the owners of Evans Limited, a massive international banking and insurance company with offices in over 50 countries and you are being a dick. I want you to leave,"

Scott laughed. He had never heard of anything so stupid in all his life.

"And stay away from our son. You are clearly a bad student with your 72s, make-up obsession and you probably have tons of other bad habits influencing our son," Joshua's mother said.

Scott just grinned because he knew Joshua's parents were far from homophobic because they had been really pleased for Harvey when he came out to them, but it would have been brilliant too if him and Joshua were in a relationship so he could count that a "nasty" habit.

Even though it was a habit he would have loved

to count.

Scott looked at sexy, beautiful Joshua and Joshua didn't dare look at him but he nodded.

Scott knew that Joshua wanted him to leave and he wondered if Joshua had ever stood up to his parents in his life.

Probably not.

But Scott had seen this all before and one day Joshua would have to make a choice. His happiness or his parents' happiness and Scott hated to imagine which one Joshua would choose.

73

CHAPTER 14

Joshua felt so guilty and like something had died inside of him as he watched Scott's cute little ass walk away from their table filled with himself, his best friend and his parents. Everyone that he loved was sitting at this table, or at least almost everyone.

The sweet aroma of mint filled his senses and Joshua just ran his fingers over the smooth white silk of the tablecloth and he couldn't understand why his parents were so hard on him. But did Scott have a point? Were his parents ruining his life?

He knew that they wouldn't care about him liking men because they were okay with Harvey, his mother had even offered to give him tips on pleasing men when he found a boyfriend. Granted Joshua never ever ever wanted *that* conversation with his mother, he would have died if she wanted to talk to him about that.

So his parents weren't destroying his life, they loved him and they only wanted what was best for him.

"That was wrong of you. Making Scott leave," Harvey said to Joshua's mother.

Joshua just looked at Harvey. What was he doing and why was he arguing? That wasn't right or fair, his parents were just trying to love him in their own special way.

"Why?" Joshua's mother asked.

"Because Joshua's been really happy at Kent University, laughing and making great friends and the research sounds like it's going to make a real difference,"

Joshua couldn't believe that even after being friends for so long Harvey still didn't know how to handle his mother, and father for that matter. Joshua knew just to let them think whatever they wanted because arguing was pointless.

Joshua's mother reached over to Harvey and rubbed his hand softly. "Darling, at Turner Limited I spend a lot of time with the Research Department because we fund a lot of research and if we funded every single proposal that *sounds* like it's going to change the world we would be bankrupt,"

Joshua didn't like where this was going.

"Anything Joshua has ever wanted to research is all theory-based. It has no practical implications so it is useless," his mother said.

Joshua couldn't take it anymore. "My brother's cancer treatment was based on biological theory. Without a theoretical understanding of how cancer works he never would have done his work,"

His mother waved him silent.

His father leant closer to Joshua and smiled. "I know you're young, you want to have fun and everything but you need to focus. You need to get your head down and really focus on these final two years because you don't want to end up like Auntie Caroline, do you?"

Joshua hated how his parents bullied Caroline for getting a degree in education and becoming a primary school teacher for Special Needs children. She transformed so many lives each year with her passion, love and dedication to her students but because she wasn't on a million pounds a year, she was a failure to the family.

"Anyway," his mother said. "When are you getting a girlfriend so we can have some grandchildren and heirs?"

Joshua knew he needed to tell them about Scott or the fact that he might be bi. Scott was so beautiful, hot and the kindest man he had ever met but he couldn't.

He just couldn't disappoint them.

"What's wrong?" his mother asked smiling. "You got a girlfriend and don't want to tell us,"

Joshua was so tempted to just say yes to get it all over with but he couldn't lie to his parents. That was one of the worst crimes a son could do.

"No mum," Joshua said, "but I'm always looking,"

"Good," his father said. "We need some young blood in the family and if you aren't going to be successful in life you might as well produce some kids for the family. We need the company to be family run in the future,"

"Why doesn't Josh run it after you two retire?" Harvey asked.

Joshua's parents exploded into laughter like that was the best joke they had ever heard.

Joshua knew that answered that question.

"Why don't you go out with Harvey one night?" his father said. "He's bi maybe he can help you pick up some girls,"

Joshua was about to smile and say that would be nice but his mother waved a hand about.

"Just remember to bring back girls please. We need heirs and as much as I love gays and bi people, you can't produce babies with guys,"

Harvey looked like he was about to say something but Joshua shot him a warning look.

"Thanks for the advice mum," Joshua said.

"Anyway baby," his mother said blowing him a kiss. "We do love you,"

Joshua loved hearing that.

"Join me for a cigarette darling," Joshua's mother said to his father.

Joshua couldn't be bothered to say anything as his parents walked away and Harvey moved closer.

"Is it me or are they getting worse?" Harvey asked.

Joshua laughed. "I just want them to be proud of me. I work hard, I do great research and I have great grades,"

"Believe me," Harvey said, "I would kill for your grades I don't know how you do it,"

"A lot of reading academic papers, critical thinking and a lot of practice," Joshua said.

"You have to tell them they need to accept Scott," Harvey said. "He really likes you and you really like him,"

"What?" Joshua asked. He couldn't imagine anything worse than telling his parents he might be bi and wanting to ask out Scott.

"What do you mean *what?* I saw you look at Scott since the moment you both walked in. Every ten seconds like clockwork you looked at him and smiled, you love him and you don't want to admit it,"

Joshua shook his head. He couldn't love another man, he couldn't do anything like that, his parents would be so disappointed in him. Everyone wanted him or one of his two brothers to create biological heirs to the family.

His two brothers were working too much to find girlfriends so it was all down to him.

Joshua gasped as he realised that for the first time, he really wasn't sure what he wanted in life. He wanted to be bi, to get a boyfriend and go out with Scott, but if he did that then he was abandoning his family. But then if he got a girlfriend, had children with her and married her like his family wanted it would be a great life but he would be leaving Scott.

And he really, really liked Scott.

Harvey huffed. "Your own neediness and damn focus on your family and studies will be your undoing,"

Joshua shook his head. "No it won't. My family love me, want the best for me and if they think I should go out with a girl then maybe I should,"

Harvey stood up and Joshua realised that he shouldn't have said any of that because it was only now he was realising he had these ideas and thoughts and opinions on everything.

Harvey frowned. "You know you are my best friend but I am not watching you throw away the best thing that could ever have happened to you because you don't have a backbone. Who gives a fuck if your parents don't approve? If they really love you like you keep banging on about they will love Scott too,"

Joshua was about to say something but Harvey simply walked away and he knew that Harvey was right. He didn't want to throw away the best thing that ever could have happened to him because both his family and Scott were important to him.

But he sadly only had another 6 days with Scott and then it would kill him inside but he could just walk away and help his family, so they would be proud of him.

Or at least Joshua really hoped they would.

CHAPTER 15

6 days later Scott was so damn excited for tonight, this was the night that he was finally going to ask out the man he loved and Joshua was going to say yes and then they would go out, be boyfriends and life would be perfect.

Everything was going to be brilliant after tonight and Scott had even cleaned his flat top to bottom, changed the bedsheets and made a restaurant reservation in the heart of Canterbury for a brilliant first date. He was so damn excited, it had been ages since he had been in a real relationship so it was so amazing that he was going to have one in less than ten minutes.

Scott leant against the bright white walls of the lab as a very tall and skinny female participant entered the house virtual environment for her last part of the experiment. She was a good participant so far and like always Joshua was a master of dealing with the participants.

He was so calm, professional and he really made the experiment fun so participants always left with a large smile on their face. Scott loved that about him.

Joshua checked the computer monitor and Scott smiled as he watched how elegantly, beautifully and perfectly Joshua just seemed to glide across the lab like an angel. He was so looking forward to exploring him and his body at some point in the future.

Joshua was so damn hot.

Scott was even happier that the Saturday night incident with Joshua's parents hadn't seemed to be a problem between them. Joshua had come into the lab and was his normal, professional and wonderful self.

It was impossible he would say no to Scott when he asked him out.

The participant jumped and Scott forced himself not to laugh.

"You're okay. The experiment is almost over," Joshua said caringly.

Scott slowly moved over to the computer monitor and grabbed the VR headset box and wet wipes that were on the chair so as soon as the participant was done he could put away the equipment, save and turn off the computer and then ask out the man he loved.

"Woo!" the woman shouted.

Scott laughed a little as he saw a massive virtual spider the size of a bed had jumped out at her.

"And we're done," Joshua said taking off the headset.

Scott took it from him and Scott loved the rough warm feeling of Joshua's fingers against his. Then as Joshua debriefed the participant he put away the VR headset and cleaned up.

"Thank you," Scott said to the participant as she left.

Scott smiled at Joshua as he grabbed his very cute cream-coloured jacket and his heartbeat increased a little but he wanted this.

Joshua smiled at him. "What?"

Scott wasn't exactly sure why he didn't know what was about to happen considering he was about to do the same, surely?

"Now we're done with the experiment, do you want to go out?" Scott asked. "Sorry that probably sounded lame but I haven't asked out a guy for ages,"

Joshua bit his lower lip and his eyes widened.

"What's wrong? You want me to do this properly," Scott said smiling. "I really like you Joshua and I would like to know you better, so will you please go on a date with me?"

Joshua gasped and looked so guilty. "I can't,"

Scott laughed and felt like someone had smashed him round the head with a spanner.

"What... what do you mean?" Scott asked forcing the words out as the whole world spun.

"I can't go out with a guy. It isn't what my family would want and I don't want to disappoint them,"

"Fuck your family! I like you. You like me. You said so!" Scott shouted.

This was outrageous. He couldn't believe this.

"And I've never been with a guy before. I think if I was going to be bi then I would have figured it out by now,"

"Like fuck would you," Scott said. "Being bi or whatever sexuality is a process, there isn't an onset date you can be bi whenever you decide,"

Joshua shook his head. "I'm sorry but I can't. Not now, not ever. But it's been a pleasure to work with-"

"Get out!" Scott shouted.

He was so done with Joshua and his stupid parents. He wanted something real, something fun and a relationship with a guy that he was falling for.

Joshua nodded and was just about to leave when he turned back and smiled.

For a stupid moment Scott wondered if Joshua was going to change his mind.

"Scott," Joshua said, "if you were a woman, I really would go on a date with you. You are beautiful and perfect,"

Then Joshua left and as much as Scott heard Joshua cry as he went down the corridor, Scott just fell against the wall and allowed his emotions and tears and rage to claim him.

CHAPTER 16

When Joshua woke up the next morning, he couldn't believe how much of an idiot he had been. He couldn't even get up out of his small lonely single bed at his parents that he was housesitting whilst they were away. He could see the slightly cold silver rays of January sunlight trying to invade the darkness of his bedroom but he didn't want to let in the light.

He had just destroyed the love of his life and Joshua knew it was an idiot.

As soon as he had forced himself home, gone through two boxes of tissues and ordered a couple of pizzas, he had collapsed into his bed and he hated himself.

Joshua had no idea how he could have been so stupid, pathetic and silly that had actually binned and shattered the heart of such a beautiful man.

"Hello," someone said.

It took a few moments until Joshua realised it was Harvey's voice and he couldn't believe that his best friend had come through for him. Joshua didn't know how Harvey knew what was happening but he was always cleverer that Joshua gave him credit for.

He heard Harvey come up the stairs and Joshua just lacked the energy to do anything. He was a heartbreaker, a needy man and he was an awful person who had thrown his happiness away for no reason.

"Wow," Harvey said pushing open the door.

It was so dark Joshua could barely see Harvey but his positivity and him just being there made Joshua smile. He forced himself to sit against his headboard and Joshua realised he had slept nude.

"Why did you do it?" Harvey asked as he sat gently on the bed knowing he was going to have to knock some sense into Josh. "Scott loved you and he would have been a great boyfriend,"

Joshua nodded. "I don't know I love my parents and I was scared,"

"You need to stand up to them,"

Joshua wanted to pace around the bedroom but he couldn't do it in the nude. He needed to find his clothes without Harvey noticing.

Harvey went over to the windows and opened the curtain. Finding his clothes without getting noticed was now impossible.

"Do your parents know?" Joshua asked.

"Of course," Harvey said. "It wasn't easy but we have a conversation, they were a little unnerved at first but after a while they understood that I was the same person who they had always loved,"

Joshua couldn't agree more. He supposed he had always been bi, he had always been able to appreciate hot, sexy men and Joshua really did love men. They were just so damn beautiful.

And he loved women too,

"How did you deal with the fear?" Joshua asked as he spotted a pair of black trunks on the floor. He needed to reach that.

"Sometimes you just need to deal with whatever's holding you back and then you need to get on with your life. You cannot let others control you forever,"

"They don't control me," Joshua said using his foot to scoop up his boxers before he put them on under the covers.

"They do. When is the last thing you *did* something for yourself? What was the last relationship you had that wasn't pre-approved by them?"

Joshua was sure he could roll off twenty off the top of his head but he couldn't. He really couldn't.

"And what would your parents say if you said you were going out with Scott?"

"That he was a bad influence," Joshua said.

"And is he?"

"Never,"

Harvey smiled as he picked up a pair of jogging bottoms and a hoody and passed them to Joshua. "Then put them on because we have work to do,"

Joshua quickly put on his clothes and he noticed that Harvey was looking at his chest as he put on his hoody and he stopped.

"Do I have a nice body?" Joshua asked. "I do as a man do I think I have?"

Harvey laughed and nodded. "Not as nice as my Jasmine but yeah, you do,"

Joshua was so glad to hear that and it sounded so nice to actually hear a guy say that about him. It just sounded so kind, natural and wonderful to hear a guy speak about him nicely.

That was why he had to fix what he had broken.

"How are we going to fix this?" Joshua asked as he got out of bed.

Harvey shrugged. "Your problem is that you don't confront your parents and your biggest problem is of what you said to Scott when you leave,"

Joshua wanted to die at the realisation Harvey knew about that.

"Why? Of all the things you could say to him why did you say, if you were a woman I would date and love you. That is basically what you said,"

Joshua had no idea but he knew he had to have a video call with his parents immediately. They were probably about to tuck into some 5-star breakfast in a hotel with a name he couldn't pronounce but that didn't matter. He was going to stand up to them and they were going to listen to him for a change.

Then he was going to beg Scott to forgive him and he had to come up with some way to prove this would never happen again.

But he had to deal with his parents first and if

they didn't like what he had to say then he could always trash their place.

Joshua couldn't deny that a large act of rebellion was a lot more exciting than he had any right to feel.

CHAPTER 17

One thing that Scott really, really liked about Steven Baker, besides from his good looks, fit as hell body and him being an amazing person was that he was seriously social. Scott offered considered him more friend than PhD student and project supervisor and that was great to know.

Scott, Steven and Delia all sat round a small metal coffee table in one of the university's other small coffee shops as the sounds of other students dragging their feet and themselves after a heavy night of drinking echoed off the bright orange walls around them.

The whooshing, banging and hissing of coffee machines filled the air and Scott was so happy when Jason joined them with his boyfriend Nick, and Scott wrapped his hands around his large coffee mug.

"That's bad mate," Steven said. "Of all the things he could have said to you, he said he could only love you if you were a woman,"

Scott laughed because it was such an outrageous thing to say.

"I never liked him," Delia said, knowing she was lying through her teeth. "I always said that bi-curious people could be a nightmare,"

Scott smiled at her. "No you don't. You really liked and you have tons of bi or curious people on your course and you love them,"

Delia mockingly threw her hands up in the air. "You see everyone you try to help him and he just smashes you down. Some friend,"

Scott blew her a kiss.

"Do you know why he said it?" Steven asked, taking a sip of his hot chocolate.

"He's scared of letting his parents down," Jason said. "

"Oh like you were when we started dating,", Nick said.

Scott leant forward and everyone did the same. He would love some domestic drama.

"I wasn't scared of what they would think. I was scared about you meeting them, I love you and I didn't want them scaring you off,"

Nick nodded. "Well it was a close one babe. I mean that mole on your mum's head was like a second eye burrowing into my rainbow heart,"

Jason playfully hit him, and Scott frowned a little. That was the sort of love, banter and jokes that he so badly wanted to have with Joshua.

"I think we need to show that Josh that he would

always be okay," Jason said. "It doesn't matter if his parents respect his choice or not, we like him and that's all that matters,"

Scott didn't have the heart to tell him that Joshua wouldn't accept that. He was too damn focused on his parents' approval.

"You know," Delia said. "Maybe giving his parents a piece of our mind help. Harvey might have their phone number,"

Scott shook his head hard as he took a gulp of his coffee. "Never. That would end so badly, like what I even say. You two are bitches and I want to love your son and you might become my in-laws and I still hate you,"

Steven laughed. "What I did to my future in-laws?"

"And it worked?" Delia asked.

"Hell no. My boyfriend broke up with me for three weeks. Worst time of my life,"

"You could become a girl?" Delia asked. "I like it,"

Everyone laughed and Scott smiled, but he felt so angry at Joshua. It was one of the most disgraceful things he had ever heard and he was fuming with Joshua was even thinking it.

Joshua was one of the most intelligent, nicest and sexiest men Scott had ever met. It was just a shame he was so obsessed with his parents' approval that he just couldn't get out of his own way when it came to his happiness.

"I'm fairly sure that process takes years," Jason said knowing this probably wasn't the best thing to say to his best friend. "And by that time Joshua might have found someone else,"

"Like a woman," Scott said.

Everyone went silent.

Scott was fairly sure his friends were meant to be helping him, not making him feel worse and worse with each word they said.

"How about we just go to London tonight?" Jason asked. "You can meet some nice boys, have hook-up sex and just have a crazy night,"

Scott wanted to say yes because at least he could forget about Joshua for a few hours but that wouldn't work. Or it might but only until he woke up tomorrow morning.

Scott stood up. "I have to tell Joshua everything I feel and think about his silly ideas and then I'm just going to forget about him. He doesn't care about me and I deserve someone who does,"

Everyone at the table nodded but they didn't dare say anything, Scott wanted one of them to say he was making the right decision he knew that he wasn't. He loved Joshua far more than he ever wanted to admit.

It was just a shame that Joshua didn't feel the same way.

CHAPTER 18

Joshua was so nervous, his hands were shaking and he felt the cold sweat roll down his back as he sat on his large wooden dining table waiting for his parents to pick up the video chat.

He was staring into the little flashing green light on his laptop as he waited and he was so glad that Harvey was sitting on the opposite side of the table to him.

And as much as Joshua didn't want to admit it, and he hadn't noticed earlier, but Harvey did look good. Nowhere near as good as Scott did, but in his tight black sportswear shorts and gym wear that highlighted his very good-looking body, Joshua couldn't deny he was definitely into men.

And women.

Joshua was relieved to finally realise all of that and he was so happy, relaxed and he felt like he had honestly discovered his true self for the first time ever. And that was an amazing feeling that he loved.

"Hello," his mother said as they answered the video chat.

She was clearly holding her phone and making sure that both his mother and father could both see him.

"Everything okay sweetheart?" his mother asked.

"Yeah, better than great mum. I have something to tell you," Joshua said.

"Honey," his mother said really hoping her son would finally get to the point and stop interrupting their breakfast. "We have a meeting with six new investors in five minutes and we're preparing for it. Unless it's life and death could you tell us later,"

"No," Joshua said, his voice cold and level. "For just once in your life listen to me, value me and love me for the son I am,"

His mother sat up perfectly straight. "I always do,"

Harvey laughed hard.

Joshua spun around the laptop before he made it focus back on him. "No you don't mum, even Harvey disagrees with you,"

"Come on son get on with it," his father said.

"Mum, Dad, I don't want a girlfriend at the moment and I don't want you to keep talking about it," Joshua said his heart pounding in his chest.

His mother nodded. "Yeah I kind of thought about that over the past week. That's wrong of us and I'm sorry we're pressuring you,"

"Thanks," Joshua said not believing he was about

to say his true feeling. "But it's also because I really like men and women. Women are beautiful but I really, really like men too,"

"I told you," his father said grinning and elbowing his mother in the ribs.

"You what?" Joshua asked.

His mother laughed. "You think we're blind. I saw how much you were smiling, laughing and looking at Scott the other night. And honestly I was horrible and I'm sorry, I think I was just shocked by it,"

Joshua could understand that, he imagined he would be shocked too if he was in his mother's shoes. She had always planned for him to be straight, have kids and have a wife. Now that might change forever.

He hoped it would.

"Scott's a nice boy," his father said.

"I second that," Harvey said.

His mother laughed. "Me too. And honestly, I think the reason why I'm so hard on you is because I'm jealous. You know our parents weren't that great and they were horrible about being poor so I suppose, I just pushed too hard to make sure you didn't experience the same,"

Joshua understood that and he had always suspected that was the reason but it still didn't make up for everything.

"And from now on, we're going to be kind, better and more loving towards you," his mother said. "And I hope you can give forgive us,"

"In time maybe," Joshua said not believing how it felt to stand up to them.

"And you must bring your boyfriend round when we return," his father said.

Joshua bit his lip and he fought back the tears that threatened to pour out of him.

"That's the problem," Harvey said coming over to the laptop. "Because silly here was so scared of you two hating him, he rejected Scott when he asked him out,"

His mother gasped. "Oh damn no this again. We must stop ruining our children's love,"

His father nodded firmly. "Right Josh, you need to go and get that man back. He loves you. You love him and he is the best thing for you and your happiness,"

Joshua laughed. He loved his parents and at least they were finally realising all the mistakes they had made.

"We're hanging up now because you need to get your boyfriend back. We love you," his mother said.

Joshua just smiled and they blew him kisses as they hung up.

Joshua stood up and was about to hug Harvey when he stepped away and smiled.

"If you want to hug a man then you hug Scott," Harvey said.

"Gladly," Joshua said.

But now he just needed to find the man he loved and beg him to forgive him after all the damage he had caused.

Something Joshua doubted even he was intelligent enough to heal. But he wanted to try no matter what.

And no matter what he had to do or prove or say. He loved Scott and he wanted to go to the ends of the earth for such a perfect man.

CHAPTER 19

Joshua had no idea how he was going to convince Scott he was sorry, he was changed and he wanted nothing more than him in the entire world. He went out the front door of his parents' house and started walking down the long wide street on the outskirts of Canterbury.

There weren't many cars parked on the road, everyone seemed to be out and all the little semi-detached houses looked the same as Joshua kept walking. He noticed that two neighbours, an elderly couple who lived a few doors up were tending to their garden. Why they were doing it in January Joshua didn't know why but he nodded at them anyway.

He had no idea where he was walking to, he was probably going to head to the bus stop at the very end of the road and go to the university that way.

Harvey had asked if he wanted a lift but Joshua wanted, needed to do this alone and he needed Scott to think that everything was his idea, and hopefully that would tell him just how sorry he was for everything.

There were a few female university students in jeans and thick fur coats on the other side of the road but Joshua didn't even bat an eyelid at them. They might have looked okay but all he cared about was Scott, and hopefully kissing those soft smooth lips that he had always wanted to taste.

A large bus honked behind him and Joshua quickened his pace in case this was the bus that could take him to the university and towards the man he loved.

The bus stopped a little earlier away from the bus stop and the most beautiful man Joshua had ever seen stepped out before the bus drove off again like it was in a high speed police chase.

Joshua just stared at Scott as they both smiled at each other. Scott was so skinny, sexy and cute that Joshua had no idea why he had been so silly. Scott had always been the one for him ever since he first saw him in Steven Baker's office.

It was always going to be him.

Joshua had never met someone as kind, hot and beautiful as Scott and now he realised he would always like men and women the same, but he was always, always meant to end up with Scott.

The man he really, really loved.

Joshua went over to him and just hugged him. He didn't care if the neighbours saw, what they thought or even what the university students walking down the road thought. He just wanted Scott to know that he loved him.

And he wasn't ashamed of liking men or wanting, needing to be with him.

"I'm sorry," Joshua said running his hands through Scott's short hair. "It's always been you, it will never be anyone else and I, I really want to date you,"

Scott didn't say anything but he didn't push away so Joshua took that as a good sign.

"I spoke to my friends, they're fine with it they want to be part of the family and they love us both,"

Scott looked at Joshua and gently stroked his cheek. "You really have changed. Would… would you want to kiss me in public?"

Scott wasn't sure if Joshua would ever agree to it but he so badly wanted the man he loved to kiss him.

"Please?" Scott asked.

Joshua laughed. "You don't have to ask me twice,"

Joshua kissed the wonderful, sexy man he had longed for, awoken his sexual desires for and as their lips met Joshua gasped in pleasure as it was the best kiss of his life. Scott's lips were soft and smooth and sweet and his stomach flipped and churned even more.

Not because he was nervous for anything but because he really knew deep down that he had always been bisexual and that was okay. It was okay and normal to like both men and women and love them both. Joshua loved Scott and that was okay as much as he would always appreciate good-looking women, he knew he wouldn't be dating one again.

Because he had Scott.

The wonderful, delightful, stunning man that had given him so much love over the past two weeks. Scott had made him realise that he was bi, he had made him stand up to his parents for the first time ever and Joshua was so glad that he now understood he didn't need to be the best student of the best to live an amazing life.

He would always have an amazing life as long as he had Scott with him, and he had a great feeling that Scott and him wouldn't be leaving each other any time soon.

CHAPTER 20

A year later a warm afternoon breeze blew through the field as Scott stood next to Delia in her big bright pink maid of honour dress, he couldn't have been more excited for what was about to happen. He was about to marry the love of his life, he was going to have a husband and everything he had ever wanted was going to be his.

Scott knew why a field on the outskirts of Canterbury might not have sounded the most romantic place for their wedding, but they were never going to have it at the university (like their parents wanted) or in a church or cathedral (like Josh's parents had wanted) but the field was perfect.

The thick lustrous green grass blew in a thick wave of green as the warm breeze blew with Canterbury and its immense cathedral spires in the background, a large brown barn was in another field for the very classy and expensive reception and everyone was so excited for the big day.

Scott loved watching all his friends and family mix with Josh's and everyone was getting on great in their long sweeping dresses in whites, blues and light mint greens. And the men looked amazing in their black and navy suits.

This was everything he had ever wanted.

He had always wanted a real, strong, loving relationship and finally beautiful Joshua was finally giving him that and Scott couldn't believe how brilliant the past year had been. It had been the best year of his life.

And it was only going to get better.

The sweet aromas of freshly cut grass, mint and vanilla filled Scott's senses making the great taste of wedding cake from the tasting sessions form on his tongue, and he was so, so excited about showing off their own wedding cake. It was amazing, not Josh amazing, but still excellent.

Scott's mum in her long pink dress popped up off the front row and just hugged him. "I'm so proud of you,"

Scott couldn't talk in case he started crying so he just hugged and kissed his mum. The woman who had moved heaven and earth and everything in-between to make sure their entire family was here for this great day.

Scott so badly wanted the wedding to start but apparently Joshua's bum crack had ripped his trousers. Scott had no problem with that whatsoever and it was only going to get ripped later on anyway.

It was pointless repairing it.

"You excited," Jason said as him and Nick and Sophia and her boyfriend came up to him.

"More than anything," Scott said and he meant every word of it.

The four of them took their seats and Scott waved at Steven Baker and his boyfriend who were married only last week take their seats and then the best man Harvey and his wife Jasmin rushed in and took their seats in the front row.

This was happening.

The band flared to life, Scott's stomach tightened as his mouth dropped as he saw his husband, the love of his life and the man he would treasure forever walk in with his mother on his arm. Nothing about the wedding was traditional but that was how Scott wanted it.

Scott had never seen Joshua look so perfect and beautiful and hot in his expensive, shiny black suit that made him look like a model on a GQ cover. Scott was so looking forward to doing him later on.

And spending the rest of their lives together.

Joshua got to the front and Scott couldn't take his eyes off him and his to-be-husband smiled back.

"I love you Scott Turner," Joshua whispered knowing that every single word of it was true. "It has always been you and I love you,"

Scott was about to say the same when Delia elbowed him and everyone laughed.

And Scott loved that the ceremony had finally

started and vows were exchanged and love was declared forever, he knew he was the luckiest man alive, because finally, finally he had true love.

Not a hook-up, not a meaningless relationship, but the real thing that he could and would treasure until the end of days or until death did them part. Scott knew both of those wouldn't be happening for a long, long time.

And it was all because he had awakened Joshua's love and he didn't regret any of it.

GET YOUR FREE SHORT STORY NOW!

And get signed up to Connor Whiteley's newsletter to hear about new gripping books, offers and exciting projects. (You'll never be sent spam)

https://www.subscribepage.com/gayromance signup

About the author:

Connor Whiteley is the author of over 60 books in the sci-fi fantasy, nonfiction psychology and books for writer's genre and he is a Human Branding Speaker and Consultant.

He is a passionate warhammer 40,000 reader, psychology student and author.

Who narrates his own audiobooks and he hosts The Psychology World Podcast.

All whilst studying Psychology at the University of Kent, England.

Also, he was a former Explorer Scout where he gave a speech to the Maltese President in August 2018 and he attended Prince Charles' 70th Birthday Party at Buckingham Palace in May 2018.

Plus, he is a self-confessed coffee lover!

Other books by Connor Whiteley:

Bettie English Private Eye Series
A Very Private Woman
The Russian Case
A Very Urgent Matter
A Case Most Personal
Trains, Scots and Private Eyes
The Federation Protects
Cops, Robbers and Private Eyes
Just Ask Bettie English
An Inheritance To Die For
The Death of Graham Adams
Bearing Witness
The Twelve
The Wrong Body
The Assassination Of Bettie English

Lord of War Origin Trilogy:
Not Scared Of The Dark
Madness
Burn Them All

The Fireheart Fantasy Series
Heart of Fire
Heart of Lies
Heart of Prophecy
Heart of Bones

Heart of Fate

<u>City of Assassins (Urban Fantasy)</u>
City of Death
City of Marytrs
City of Pleasure
City of Power

<u>Agents of The Emperor</u>
Return of The Ancient Ones
Vigilance
Angels of Fire
Kingmaker
The Eight
The Lost Generation
Hunt
Emperor's Council
Speaker of Treachery
Birth Of The Empire
Terraforma

<u>The Rising Augusta Fantasy Adventure Series</u>
Rise To Power
Rising Walls
Rising Force
Rising Realm

<u>Lord Of War Trilogy (Agents of The Emperor)</u>
Not Scared Of The Dark
Madness
Burn It All Down

<u>Gay Romance Novellas</u>
Breaking, Nursing, Repairing A Broken Heart
Jacob And Daniel
Fallen For A Lie
Spying And Weddings

<u>Miscellaneous:</u>
RETURN
FREEDOM
SALVATION
Reflection of Mount Flame
The Masked One
The Great Deer
English Independence

OTHER SHORT STORIES BY CONNOR WHITELEY

<u>Mystery Short Story Collections</u>
Criminally Good Stories Volume 1: 20 Detective Mystery Short Stories
Criminally Good Stories Volume 2: 20 Private Investigator Short Stories
Criminally Good Stories Volume 3: 20 Crime Fiction Short Stories
Criminally Good Stories Volume 4: 20 Science Fiction and Fantasy Mystery Short Stories
Criminally Good Stories Volume 5: 20 Romantic Suspense Short Stories

<u>Mystery Short Stories:</u>
Protecting The Woman She Hated
Finding A Royal Friend
Our Woman In Paris
Corrupt Driving
A Prime Assassination
Jubilee Thief
Jubilee, Terror, Celebrations
Negative Jubilation
Ghostly Jubilation
Killing For Womenkind
A Snowy Death

Miracle Of Death
A Spy In Rome
The 12:30 To St Pancreas
A Country In Trouble
A Smokey Way To Go
A Spicy Way To GO
A Marketing Way To Go
A Missing Way To Go
A Showering Way To Go
Poison In The Candy Cane
Kendra Detective Mystery Collection Volume 1
Kendra Detective Mystery Collection Volume 2
Mystery Short Story Collection Volume 1
Mystery Short Story Collection Volume 2
Criminal Performance
Candy Detectives
Key To Birth In The Past

Science Fiction Short Stories:
Their Brave New World
Gummy Bear Detective
The Candy Detective
What Candies Fear
The Blurred Image
Shattered Legions

The First Rememberer
Life of A Rememberer
System of Wonder
Lifesaver
Remarkable Way She Died
The Interrogation of Annabella Stormic
Blade of The Emperor
Arbiter's Truth
Computation of Battle
Old One's Wrath
Puppets and Masters
Ship of Plague
Interrogation
Edge of Failure

<u>Fantasy Short Stories:</u>
City of Snow
City of Light
City of Vengeance
Dragons, Goats and Kingdom
Smog The Pathetic Dragon
Don't Go In The Shed
The Tomato Saver
The Remarkable Way She Died
Dragon Coins
Dragon Tea
Dragon Rider

All books in 'An Introductory Series':
Careers In Psychology
Psychology of Suicide
Dementia Psychology
Clinical Psychology Reflections Volume 4
Forensic Psychology of Terrorism And Hostage-Taking
Forensic Psychology of False Allegations
Year In Psychology
CBT For Anxiety
CBT For Depression
Applied Psychology
BIOLOGICAL PSYCHOLOGY 3RD EDITION
COGNITIVE PSYCHOLOGY THIRD EDITION
SOCIAL PSYCHOLOGY- 3RD EDITION
ABNORMAL PSYCHOLOGY 3RD EDITION
PSYCHOLOGY OF RELATIONSHIPS- 3RD EDITION
DEVELOPMENTAL PSYCHOLOGY 3RD EDITION
HEALTH PSYCHOLOGY
RESEARCH IN PSYCHOLOGY
A GUIDE TO MENTAL HEALTH AND TREATMENT AROUND THE WORLD-

A GLOBAL LOOK AT DEPRESSION
FORENSIC PSYCHOLOGY
THE FORENSIC PSYCHOLOGY OF THEFT, BURGLARY AND OTHER CRIMES AGAINST PROPERTY
CRIMINAL PROFILING: A FORENSIC PSYCHOLOGY GUIDE TO FBI PROFILING AND GEOGRAPHICAL AND STATISTICAL PROFILING.
CLINICAL PSYCHOLOGY
FORMULATION IN PSYCHOTHERAPY
PERSONALITY PSYCHOLOGY AND INDIVIDUAL DIFFERENCES
CLINICAL PSYCHOLOGY REFLECTIONS VOLUME 1
CLINICAL PSYCHOLOGY REFLECTIONS VOLUME 2
Clinical Psychology Reflections Volume 3
CULT PSYCHOLOGY
Police Psychology

A Psychology Student's Guide To University
How Does University Work?
A Student's Guide To University And Learning
University Mental Health and Mindset

www.ingramcontent.com/pod-product-compliance
Lightning Source LLC
LaVergne TN
LVHW011844060526
838200LV00054B/4153